Stacey
the Soccer
Fairy

Special thanks to
Narinder Dhami

ISBN 978-0-545-20253-4

Copyright © 2008 by Rainbow Magic Limited.

Previously published as *Francesca the Football Fairy* by Orchard U.K. in 2008.

All rights reserved. Published by Scholastic Inc., 557 Broadway, New York, NY 10012, by arrangement with Rainbow Magic Limited.

12 11 10 9 8 7 6 5 4 3 2   10 11 12 13 14 15/0

Printed in the U.S.A.   40

First Scholastic Printing, April 2010

Stacey
the Soccer
Fairy

by Daisy Meadows

SCHOLASTIC INC.

New York   Toronto   London   Auckland

Sydney   Mexico City   New Delhi   Hong Kong

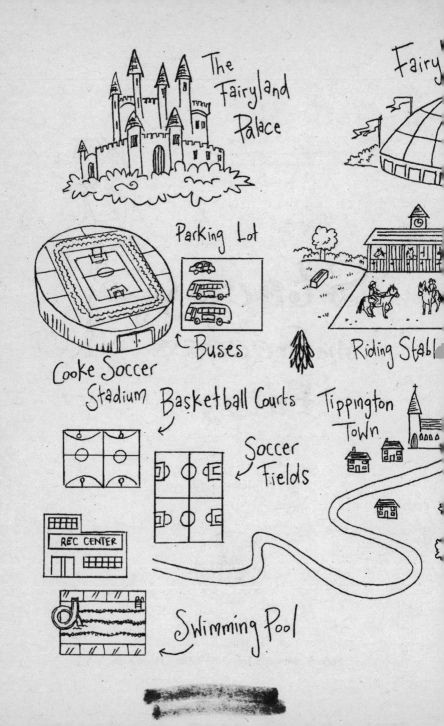

The Fairyland Palace

Fairy

Parking Lot

Buses

Cooke Soccer Stadium

Riding Stabl

Basketball Courts

Tippington Town

Soccer Fields

REC CENTER

Swimming Pool

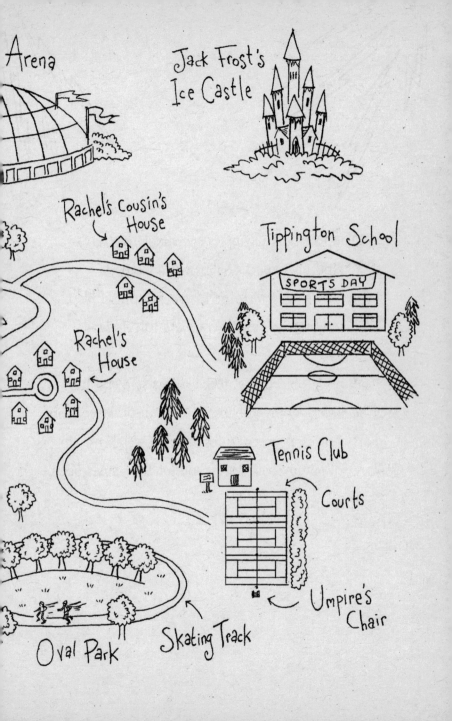

Arena

Jack Frost's
Ice Castle

Rachel's Cousin's
House

Tippington School

SPORTS DAY

Rachel's
House

Tennis Club

Courts

Oval Park

Skating Track

Umpire's
Chair

The Fairyland Olympics are about to start,
And my expert goblins will take part.
We will win this year, for I have a cunning plan.
I'll send my goblins to compete in Fairyland.

The magic objects that make sports safe and fun
Will be stolen by my goblins, to keep until we've won.
Sports Fairies, prepare to lose and to watch us win.
Goblins, follow my commands, and let the games begin!

Contents

Soccer Superstars

"You look great, Dad!" Rachel Walker laughed, glancing at her father as she climbed out of the car. Mr. Walker was wearing a blue-and-white soccer jersey and scarf, his face was painted with blue and white stripes, and he had a fluffy blue-and-white wig on his head.

"The wig's fantastic!" Kirsty Tate, Rachel's best friend, added with a grin. She was staying with the Walkers over spring vacation. "He's going to be the best-dressed Tippington Rovers fan here."

Rachel nodded. "I'm glad Mom and I are just wearing scarves, though," she added. "That wig looks kind of warm!"

"It is, but I want to show my support

for the team," said Mr. Walker, as they left the parking lot and joined the other soccer fans heading toward the Cooke Stadium. "This is a very important game, girls. If Tippington beats the Compton Capitals today, the team will be moved up to the next league!"

Rachel and Kirsty exchanged concerned glances. They were both worried that the soccer game would be a complete disaster, because the Sports Fairies had lost their magic objects! When these special objects were in their proper places—either with the Sports

Fairies or in the fairies' lockers—they ensured that sports in both the human and fairy worlds were safe, fun, and exciting. Unfortunately, the objects had been stolen by the mischievous Jack Frost and his goblins.

Jack Frost was determined to win the Fairyland Olympics, which started in just six days. He knew his team needed the objects to win, so he had ordered his goblins to hide them in the human world until the games took place. By keeping the magic objects close to them, the goblins would win every single event. The Fairyland Olympics couldn't be cancelled, because that would ruin the Olympic Games in the human world, too. Rachel and Kirsty had promised their fairy friends that they would do

their best to find the objects before the
games.

"I'm glad we persuaded Mom and
Dad to come to the game early today,"
Rachel said quietly to Kirsty. "Maybe
the goblin who has Stacey the Soccer
Fairy's magic soccer ball will be here,
too."

"Helena the
Horse-riding Fairy
did say that any
goblin who has one
of the magic objects
will want to be near
that sport," Kirsty
agreed. The girls
had helped Helena get her magic riding
helmet back just the day before. "She
also said that Jack Frost told the goblins

to practice their sports skills before the Fairyland Olympics."

"Yes, and King Oberon said that the winning Olympic team will get the Fairyland Olympic Cup, which is filled with luck," Kirsty reminded Rachel. "Think how much more trouble Jack Frost could cause if he had lots of good luck!"

"Girls, come get your picture taken," called Mrs. Walker, holding up her camera.

"Oh, good idea," Rachel said, as she and Kirsty hurried over to join her parents outside the stadium entrance. "Then we won't forget how much work Dad put into his outfit!"

"I feel like the odd one out," Kirsty joked, as Mrs. Walker took their photo.

"I'm the only one not wearing any
Tippington Rovers colors."

"There's a souvenir booth inside the
stadium," Rachel's dad told her. "We'll
buy you a scarf there."

"Thank you!" Kirsty exclaimed.

As they went inside the stadium,

Rachel immediately started looking for any sign of goblins, but she didn't see any flashes of goblin green.

Remember, you have to let the magic come to you, Rachel told herself. But she couldn't help hoping that the magic would come before the game started. Otherwise, the game would be ruined!

There weren't many people inside the stadium yet, so there wasn't a line at the souvenir booth. They headed straight to it, and Mr. Walker bought a scarf for Kirsty.

"Here you are, dear," said the cashier, dropping the scarf into a shopping bag and handing it to Kirsty. "Enjoy the game."

"Thank you," Kirsty said gratefully.

"Let's go and find our seats," Mrs.
Walker suggested.

They all went into the main part
of the stadium, which was still fairly
empty. Kirsty and Rachel had the
chance to take a good look around,
but neither of the girls could see
anything out of the ordinary.

"Maybe we should explore," Kirsty

whispered to Rachel. "There may be goblin mischief going on somewhere else."

"Dad, is it OK if Kirsty and I go look around?" asked Rachel.

"That's fine," Mr. Walker replied, getting comfortable in his seat. "We'll sit and watch the pre-game coverage on the giant TV screens."

"Just make sure you're back before the game starts," Rachel's mom added.

The girls nodded.

"I'll put my new scarf on," Kirsty said, as she and Rachel hurried off. She opened the bag, and a cloud of glittering sparkles immediately burst from inside. As both girls stared in surprise, the scarf rose gracefully from the bag, with a tiny fairy perched daintily on the end of it!

Commentary Confusion

"It's Stacey the Soccer Fairy!" Kirsty cried in delight.

"Hello, girls!" Stacey called. She wore a green-and-yellow soccer jersey with matching shorts and soccer cleats. Her long hair was braided and tied back in a ponytail. She hovered in the air in front of the girls as the scarf wrapped gently

around Kirsty's neck. "I have a feeling
those very pesky goblins may be here!"
she added.

"We've been looking for them," Rachel
told her, "but we haven't seen any yet."

Suddenly, one of the stadium officials
came running toward them. Stacey
quickly hid behind a fold of Kirsty's scarf,
but the official was too busy speaking
into a walkie-talkie to notice her.

"Yes, all the soccer balls in the stadium have vanished!" he exclaimed. "If we don't find one soon, the game will have to be cancelled!" With that, he disappeared into the players' locker room.

"Hmm. Missing soccer balls! This has goblin mischief written all over it," Stacey said.

"But why would a goblin have taken all the soccer balls?" asked Rachel, confused.

"Yes, if he has your magic soccer ball, why would he need any others?" Kirsty asked.

"I don't know," Stacey replied.

"Well, let's see if we can find the goblin and get the soccer balls back," Rachel suggested.

Just then, one of the giant TV screens overhead caught Kirsty's attention. "Rachel, look," she cried. "There's your dad!"

Rachel glanced up and her face broke into a smile. Mr. Walker was on the TV

screen, being interviewed by a sports commentator. "So, Mr. Walker, what do you think will happen in the game today?" asked the commentator. "Oh, the Tippington Rovers will win!" Rachel's dad

16

replied confidently. "I think the score will be two to zero."

"Your dad's wig looks great on camera, Rachel!" Stacey giggled.

The commentator thanked Mr. Walker, turned away, and headed through the stadium, still talking to the camera.

"OK, girls," Stacey said. "Where should we search for the goblins?"

Just as Kirsty was about to look away from the TV screen, the commentator opened the door of his broadcasting booth. Kirsty noticed that there was someone inside. A small person wearing a tracksuit, a wool Tippington Rovers hat, and a red Compton Capitols scarf was sitting on the floor. He was searching through a big mesh bag filled with soccer balls.

"Oh, hello," said the commentator, sounding surprised. "Are you here to cover the game with me?"

Curiously, Kirsty stared up at the screen, wondering why all the soccer balls were stashed away in the broadcast booth.

The small man looked up grumpily at the commentator. As he did, the scarf, which was wrapped around the bottom of his face, slipped. Kirsty caught a glimpse of green.

"Oh!" she gasped. "There's the goblin!"

"Where?" Rachel and Stacey both said together, looking around.

"Up there," Kirsty told them, pointing at the TV. "He's in the broadcast booth with all the soccer balls!"

As Rachel and Stacey glanced up at the screen, the goblin pulled his scarf quickly back into place, but not before Rachel had spotted a green, pointy nose.

"It *is* the goblin," she agreed. "And he looks so silly, wearing both Tippington and Compton colors!"

"Let's head for the broadcast booth right now," Stacey called, already flying into the air. "If the goblin's there, then I bet my magic soccer ball is, too!"

Soccer Balls Galore

Stacey and the girls rushed over to the broadcast booth. Even though they couldn't keep their eyes on the TV screens as they ran, they could still hear the commentator over the stadium's loudspeaker. He was trying to talk to the goblin.

"So, Mr. . . . um . . ." said the commentator, sounding confused. "Did you say what your name was?"

"No," the goblin snapped rudely.

"Well, who do you think is going to win the game?" the commentator asked.

"Um . . ." There was a long silence.

". . . The United States?" the goblin said hesitantly. "Brazil?"

Stacey, Rachel, and Kirsty couldn't help laughing.

"Those teams aren't even playing here today!" the commentator said with frustration. "This isn't the World Cup."

"Well, that was a silly question anyway," the goblin declared with a loud sniff.

"The broadcast booth is just around

the corner," Rachel panted, pointing at a
sign on the wall.

Soon the girls were at the bottom of
a flight of stairs that led up to the back
of the broadcast booth. Luckily, there
was no one else around.

"What do we do now?" asked Kirsty.

They were near another one of the giant
TV screens. Rachel glanced up at it.

BROADCAST BOOTH

The commentator was stammering, "Okay, and, um . . . now back to the studio!" Meanwhile, the goblin swung the door of the booth open and began to stomp out, dragging the bag of soccer balls behind him.

"The goblin's coming!" Rachel exclaimed, pointing to the top of the stairs.

The girls started up the steps. They saw the goblin appear above them with the mesh bag of soccer balls.

"STOP RIGHT THERE!"
Stacey shouted.

Startled, the goblin jumped
and let go
of the bag. All
the balls tumbled out of
it, bouncing down the
steps toward the girls.

"It's raining soccer
balls!" Rachel
gasped, trying to
dodge the balls.

"Look out for
Stacey's magic
soccer ball, Rachel!"
Kirsty called, darting
from side to side.

"That's fancy footwork,
girls!" Stacey called

approvingly as Kirsty and Rachel
sidestepped the flying soccer balls.
The goblin was rushing down the
steps toward them now, trying
to gather the black-and-white
balls up in his arms.
Then Rachel noticed that
one of the soccer balls
heading toward her was
surrounded by tiny
golden sparkles.
Stacey's magic soccer ball!
Rachel thought, her
heart pounding
with excitement.
She reached out
for the special ball,
but the goblin had spotted it
at exactly the same moment.

He dropped the other balls immediately and ran after Stacey's ball.

"Get out of my way!" the goblin yelled, shoving Rachel aside. She stumbled, and the magic soccer ball bounced past her. The goblin wildly grabbed at it, but missed.

The soccer ball bounced to the bottom

of the steps, and Rachel and the goblin both raced after it. But at that very moment, one of the stadium officials came around the corner. He spotted the magic soccer ball and instantly scooped it up into his arms.

So Near and Yet So Far

"Oh no!" Rachel gasped, dismayed. She glanced at her fairy friend.

Luckily, Stacey had managed to duck out of sight as soon as the official appeared, and she was now peeking anxiously out from behind a lock of Kirsty's hair.

"What's going on here?" the official asked sternly, staring at the goblin.

"We've been searching for these soccer balls everywhere. A ballboy is supposed to look after the balls, not lose them!"

The official thinks the goblin is a ballboy! Rachel realized. *He must be wearing one of the official ballboy outfits.*

"Pick up all these soccer balls, please," the official went on.

Scowling, the goblin did as he was told. He shoved the soccer balls back into the bag one by one. Rachel and Kirsty began to help. *Maybe we'll still have a chance to get the magic soccer ball back,* Kirsty thought hopefully.

"Oh, don't bother with that, girls," the official said with a smile. "The game will be starting soon, and you don't want to miss it. You should go find your seats."

Reluctantly, Rachel and Kirsty moved away. They watched as the official put the magic soccer ball into the mesh bag with the others. Then he took the bag from the goblin and headed down a corridor that led to the back of the stadium.

"Come on," he said to the goblin. "We need to find the other ballboys and girls."

The goblin smirked at Kirsty and Rachel before skipping off after the official.

"Oh no!" Stacey flew out from behind Kirsty's hair, looking very sad. "Where's he taking my ball? We have to get it back!"

"That's going to be tough," Kirsty said with a frown. She pointed at a sign on the wall of the corridor that read: PRIVATE—NO PUBLIC ACCESS. "We aren't allowed into the official areas of the stadium. The goblin's only allowed in because that man thinks he's a ballboy."

Stacey winked at her. "Well, with a little bit of magic, anything's possible. Maybe they could use a couple more

ballgirls?" She
waved her wand
and, in a shower
of dazzling fairy
dust, Kirsty and
Rachel's outfits
changed. Now
they were both
wearing dark blue
tracksuits, exactly like the goblin's.

"Let's go!" Rachel cried.

The three friends hurried down the
hallway. They couldn't see the goblin or
the official, so they began checking the
rooms along the corridor. They peeked
inside them, but there was no sign of the
goblin or the soccer balls.

As they got near a turn in the corridor,

they heard voices coming from a room. Its
door was open.

Rachel and Kirsty peeked around the
door. Inside, they could see a large group
of ballboys and ballgirls. Each of them
held a soccer ball, and they were listening
closely to a man at the front of the
room.

"And remember, it's important to

get the ball back into play as soon as possible," the man was saying.

Kirsty nudged Rachel. "There's the mesh bag that held the soccer balls," she whispered, pointing at the bag that was now lying empty on the floor.

"But where's Stacey's magic soccer ball?" Rachel whispered back, searching all the balls in the room for the telltale sparkle of fairy magic. "Nobody in here seems to have it."

"The goblin's not here either," Stacey said with a frown. "He must have gotten away with my ball."

"We'd better go," Kirsty murmured. "Otherwise, that official might see us and call us into the meeting."

The girls slipped away quietly and headed down the hall.

"Where should we look for the goblin now?" asked Rachel.

The girls stared at each other in desperation. All of a sudden, they heard a croaky voice singing a soccer cheer:

"Go, goblins, go!
Kick it high,
Kick it low.

Win, goblins, win!
Crush their toes,
Kick their shins."

"'Kick their shins'? That's not a very nice cheer," Rachel said.

"Then it's the goblin, for sure!" Stacey cried.

Soccer Showdown

"After him!" Kirsty shouted.

Stacey and the girls darted around the hall corner. Ahead of them, they saw the goblin. He was still singing to himself in his croaky voice. He was running along and expertly dribbling a soccer ball ahead of him, occasionally flicking the ball up with his toe and then heading it forward.

"Wow!" Rachel panted as they chased after him. "He's better than some of the Tippington Rovers players!"

"That's the magic of my soccer ball at work," Stacey told her.

"He's getting away from us even though he's dribbling that soccer ball," Kirsty pointed out as the goblin headed toward a door at the end of the corridor.

"Girls, you'll be much faster if you're fairy-size." Stacey said, raising her wand.

Rachel and Kirsty skidded to a halt, and Stacey showered them with fairy dust. They instantly shrank to become tiny fairies, with glittering wings on their backs!

As Stacey and the girls swiftly flew down the hallway together, the goblin swung the door open and skipped outside. He didn't even bother  to close the door behind him again.

A moment later, Stacey, Kirsty,

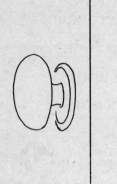

and Rachel reached the door and peeked outside. "Oh, it's the stadium parking lot!" Rachel exclaimed. "But where's the goblin?" asked Kirsty, staring at all the buses and cars parked in neat rows. A lot more soccer fans were arriving now. It was getting close to the start of the game!

"He must be somewhere in the parking lot," Stacey decided. "We'll have to search for him, but we can't let anyone see us."

Rachel and Kirsty nodded and

followed Stacey high up into the air.
They hovered above the parking lot
so they could get a good view of
everything below them, but they saw no
sign of the goblin anywhere!

"Maybe we should split up and search
each part of the parking lot more
carefully," Kirsty suggested.

Rachel was about to reply when a strange sight caught her eye. A bus was heading very slowly toward one of the parking lot exits, zig-zagging from side to side.

"Look at that bus," Rachel said to her friends. "Why is it leaving before the game has even started?"

"That's strange," Stacey agreed.

"Let's check it out," Kirsty suggested, zooming downward.

Rachel and Stacey followed. As the three of them drew even with the bus, they peeked through the windows.

"It's full of goblins!" Kirsty cried, looking up and down the packed bus.

"What are they doing here?" asked Rachel anxiously.

"It's the Goblin Olympic Soccer Team," Stacey explained, looking worried. "They must all be hoping to practice with my magic soccer ball."

The goblins were dressed in white
jerseys that had a picture of Jack Frost
on the front. They all looked extremely
proud of themselves, bouncing up and
down in their seats, and singing loudly:

> *"Go, goblins, go!*
> *Kick it high,*
> *Kick it low.*
>
> *Win, goblins, win!*
> *Crush their toes,*
> *Kick their shins."*

"They're not very sportsmanlike, are they?" Stacey said, frowning. "Soccer players never kick shins on purpose."

"But where's the goblin with the magic soccer ball?" asked Kirsty.

Rachel soon spotted him. The goblin they'd been chasing was now driving the bus, his face creased in concentration.

"Look, girls," Stacey whispered, pointing her wand at the goblins' feet. Rachel and Kirsty glanced down and saw the magic soccer ball rolling around on the floor of the bus.

"Let's find

somewhere else to practice our soccer skills," shouted the goblin driver to the rest of the team.

"We've wasted lots of time, though," moaned a goblin at the back of the bus. "Just because you got the magic soccer ball mixed up with a lot of the humans' soccer balls."

"Well, I found it again, didn't I?" the goblin at the wheel answered. "Anyway, I was just checking out the stadium to find somewhere for us to practice. I didn't know some silly humans were going to be playing a game here today!"

"Can't you drive any faster?"
demanded another goblin.

"At this rate we won't get out of the
parking lot before the Fairyland Olympics
start in six days!" another added.

"Oh, be quiet!" the goblin at the wheel
snapped. "We've got the magic soccer
ball, and that's all that matters. Those
pesky fairies won't stand a chance of
beating us in the Fairyland Olympics!"

The goblins cheered loudly.
Meanwhile, Stacey, Rachel, and Kirsty
looked at one
another with
concern.

"How are we
going to get the
magic soccer ball
back?" Kirsty

whispered as they hovered beside the slow-moving bus. "There are too many goblins around!"

Rachel thought for a moment. "Maybe we can distract the driver while Stacey sneaks onto the bus and gets her soccer ball," she suggested.

"Good idea," Stacey agreed. "When I try to pick up the ball, it will immediately shrink to its Fairyland size. It's going to be difficult for me to get close to it while it's rolling around on the floor of the bus. You'll have to buy me as much time as you can, girls."

"We will!" Kirsty said in a determined voice.

Stacey pointed her wand at the driver's window and, with a few sparkles of fairy magic, it slid open a crack.

"Good luck, girls," Stacey whispered as the three of them quickly zipped in through the open window.

Kirsty and Rachel both felt very nervous as they watched Stacey zoom down toward the magic ball. Would their plan work?

Go Home, Goblins!

"Let's give this goblin a surprise, Kirsty," Rachel whispered.

Kirsty nodded, and followed Rachel. The two fairy friends landed on top of the steering wheel.

"Hello!" Rachel called, waving up at the goblin.

"Remember us?" Kirsty added.

The goblin's eyes almost popped out of their sockets. "Are you girls or fairies?" he asked, scratching his head in confusion. Then he let out a cry of rage. "Ooh, you're both!" He took his hands off the steering wheel and began swatting furiously at the girls.

As Rachel and Kirsty dodged out of his way, the bus began to swerve wildly. Kirsty glanced down and saw that the magic soccer ball was rolling around all over the place. Stacey couldn't get close to it at all!

"Look out!" Rachel gasped suddenly, as she saw that the bus was heading right for a row of parked cars.

"Hit the brakes!" Kirsty shouted.

Looking scared, the goblin slammed on the brakes. The bus jerked to a halt, barely nudging one of the cars on its bumper. Rachel, Kirsty, and the goblins breathed sighs of relief.

"Don't panic!" the goblin driver shouted. "I have everything under control."

But, at that very moment, the airbag

inside the steering wheel
inflated. It got bigger
and bigger until it
covered the
goblin's head.

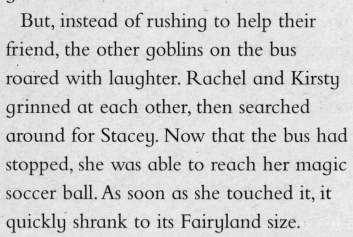

"Help!" sputtered
the goblin. "I've
been attacked by a
giant balloon!"

But, instead of rushing to help their
friend, the other goblins on the bus
roared with laughter. Rachel and Kirsty
grinned at each other, then searched
around for Stacey. Now that the bus had
stopped, she was able to reach her magic
soccer ball. As soon as she touched it, it
quickly shrank to its Fairyland size.

With a bright smile, Stacey scooped

up her precious soccer ball and zoomed
upward to join Rachel and Kirsty.
"Thanks, girls!" Stacey laughed. "Now,
let's get out of here."

The three of them fluttered through the
open window again, just as the driver-
goblin struggled free of the airbag. He
glanced down and scowled when he saw
that the soccer ball was gone.

"Those fairies stole the magic soccer ball!" he shouted.

The goblins scrambled off the bus as quickly as they could to race after Stacey and the girls. The three fairies hovered in midair, just out of reach.

"You goblins had better go home and start practicing your soccer skills," Stacey said sternly. "Because now you won't have the magic soccer ball to help you!"

The goblins grumbled and moaned when they saw the sparkling soccer ball tucked safely under Stacey's arm.

"Why didn't you stop them from taking the ball?" shouted the driver-goblin to his friends.

"Don't blame us!" the other goblins insisted. "This is all your fault!"

"Off you go, back to Fairyland," said Stacey.

The goblins muttered grumpily and stuck out their tongues at Stacey and the girls as they stomped off.

"They have a lot of soccer practicing to do now," Stacey said with a grin. "But if they do win at the Fairyland Olympics, at least they'll

have won fair and square. Now I need
to go right back to Fairyland and tell
everyone the good news. But first, there
are a few things I must make right. . . ."

Stacey touched the magic soccer ball
with her wand, and a sparkling burst of
 golden light
fizzed briefly
around it. Rachel
and Kirsty
watched as
Stacey checked
that the car the
bus had bumped
into wasn't damaged. Then she pointed
her wand at the bus. A burst of fairy dust
surrounded it, rolling it gently back into
an empty parking space.

Finally, Stacey led Rachel and Kirsty

back into the stadium. There, another cloud of fairy dust turned the girls back to their normal sizes and returned them to their original outfits.

"Thank you again, girls," Stacey said, her eyes twinkling. "Everything will be fine with the game between Tippington and Compton now, and it's just about to start. Go and have a good time!"

Rachel and Kirsty waved as Stacey flew high above their heads. "Good-bye," they called.

Stacey waved back and blew the girls a kiss. Then, with a sly smile, she began dribbling her magic soccer ball from toe to toe in midair. The next second, she

and the ball both vanished in a cloud of
fairy sparkles.

"Now we can really enjoy the game,
Kirsty," Rachel said happily as they
rushed back to their seats. "It's great to
know that Stacey has her soccer ball
back."

Kirsty grinned and nodded. "Yes—and
let's hope the Tippington Rovers win!"
she cheered.

Now Rachel and Kirsty need to help

Zoe the Skating Fairy!

Jack Frost's goblins have stolen
Zoe's magic lace. Can Rachel and
Kirsty help Zoe get it back?

Join their next adventure in this
special sneak peek!

Skating Struggles

Rachel Walker held on tightly to the
railing as she stood up on her in-line
skates. "Whoa-a-a!" She laughed, as her
feet rolled in different directions. "How are
you doing, Kirsty?"

Kirsty Tate, Rachel's best friend, was still
sitting on the grass, tying the laces on her
skates. She fastened the top straps, then

smiled up at Rachel. Kirsty was staying with Rachel's family for a week during the spring break, and today the girls had come to Oval Park, near the Walkers' house.

"All right . . . I think," Kirsty replied, clutching Rachel's hand and standing up. Then she grinned. "We must be crazy to be skating today after everything that's happened with the Sports Fairies," she said, wobbling on her wheels.

"At least we'll be nice and safe," Rachel reminded her, tapping on Kirsty's helmet. "And this is such a good place to skate, I'm sure we'll still have fun."

Unfortunately, the skaters and skateboarders seemed to be getting lots of bumps and bruises today. Kirsty and Rachel watched as a boy on a skateboard mistimed a jump, and fell off his board onto the grass

nearby. He wasn't hurt but he looked
very confused. "Why can't I do that jump
today?" they heard him mutter to himself.

The girls exchanged glances. They knew
why he was struggling with the jump.
It was because Zoe the Skating Fairy's
magic lace was missing. That meant
skaters and skateboarders everywhere were
having trouble!

RAINBOW magic™

There's Magic in Every Series!

The Rainbow Fairies

The Weather Fairies

The Jewel Fairies

The Pet Fairies

The Fun Day Fairies

The Petal Fairies

The Dance Fairies

The Music Fairies

The Sports Fairies

The Party Fairies

Read them all!

■ SCHOLASTIC

www.scholastic.com
www.rainbowmagiconline.com

HiT entertainment

RMFAIRY

RAINBOW magic™

THE RAINBOW FAIRIES

Find the magic in every book!

SCHOLASTIC
www.scholastic.com
www.rainbowmagiconline.com

HIT entertainment

RAINBOW

SPECIAL EDITION

Three Books in One!
More Rainbow Magic Fun!

Joy
the Summer
Vacation
Fairy

by Daisy Meadows

Holly
the Christmas
Fairy

by Daisy Meadows

Kylie
the Carnival
Fairy

by Daisy Meadows

Stella
the Star
Fairy

by Daisy Meadows

Shannon
the Ocean
Fairy

by Daisy Meadows

Trixie
the Halloween
Fairy

by Daisy Meadows

Gabriella
the Snow Kingdom
Fairy

by Daisy
Meadows

Juliet
the Valentine
Fairy

by Daisy Meadows

SCHOLASTIC
www.scholastic.com
www.rainbowmagiconline.com

HIT entertainment

RMSPECIAL2